Crash

SADDLEBACK™
EDUCATIONAL PUBLISHING

T H E   H E I G H T S ™

Blizzard River

Camp Sail

Crash Score

Dive Swamp

Neptune Twister

Original text by Ed Hansen
Adapted by Mary Kate Doman

SADDLEBACK™
EDUCATIONAL PUBLISHING
www.sdlback.com

ISBN-13: 978-1-61651-283-5
ISBN-10: 1-61651-283-0
eBook: 978-1-60291-697-5

Printed in Guangzhou, China
0811/CA21101347

16 15 14 13 12   2 3 4 5 6

Chapter 1

Rafael Silva was at work. It was
his last day before vacation. He
was looking forward to time off. He
wanted to spend time at home in the
Heights. He missed his family. Then
the phone rang. He picked it up.

"Hello," he sighed.

"Is this Rafael Silva?" the man on
the phone asked.

"Yes," Rafael replied.

"This is Jack Wheeler. I own a company in California. We need a new building. And we need it fast. Can you help?"

"I would like to," Rafael said. "But I am going on vacation."

"That's okay. You can start after," Jack said.

Then Jack Wheeler had an idea. The Silvas should vacation in California.

"You can come to California. Bring the family. And you can stop by. You can see my company," he said. "I have a plane. I will fly you here. I will pay for the hotel."

"That's very nice," Rafael said.

"There's a lot to do here," Jack said. "It's a fun place."

Rafael was happy. His kids would like Jack's plane. Ana was in Mexico with her parents. He said yes.

It was the next day. It was time for vacation. The Silvas were at the airport. They were waiting for the plane. A car pulled up. A man got out. He was big. He was over six feet tall. He had long, black hair. The Silvas looked at each other. They looked scared.

The man smiled. "Hello," he said. "Are you the Silvas? I'm Johnny. Johnny Hightower. I'm your pilot."

"Yes," said Rafael. "We're the Silvas. These are my kids."

Lilia, Antonio, and Franco said hello.

Eleven-year-old Lilia looked at

Johnny. "Where's the plane?" she asked.

"Over there," said Johnny. He pointed to a small, silver plane.

"Looks small," Antonio said.

Johnny laughed. "It's big inside. We'll all fit. I fly this plane every day. And I'm a big guy."

Everyone walked to the plane. They loaded their bags. Then they got inside. Johnny was right. The plane was big. Soon they were in the air. They looked out the window. The plane flew high. Everything looked small.

Franco read a book. Antonio played his DS. Lilia took a nap. Rafael looked at his kids. Only Ana was missing.

They flew for hours. Rafael looked out the window. The sky was dark. It looked like a storm.

"Oh man!" Johnny yelled.

Rafael jumped. "What's wrong?" he asked.

"It's a storm. It's a big storm. We're headed for it!" Johnny said.

Lilia screamed.

"It's okay Lilia," Rafael said calmly.

"Your dad's right. It will be okay. We'll fly over it," said Johnny.

The storm got bigger. Clouds were everywhere. The small plane headed into the storm.

Chapter 2

Rain hit the plane. It was loud.
Everyone looked scared. They were
afraid to look out the windows. But
Franco looked. He saw lightning. He
heard thunder.

"This is a big storm," Franco said.

It was windy. The plane shook.

"What if the wings fall off?"
Antonio gasped.

"They won't," said Franco.

"How do you know? You can't tell," argued Antonio.

"Boys! Stop fighting!" yelled Rafael. "Johnny needs our help."

Lightning lit the sky. The thunder was loud. The lights went out. The plane went dark. Then the plane fell.

"The lightning hit us!" Lilia yelled.

The Silvas looked scared. Johnny looked scared. The plane was going down! The storm was loud! It was very dark!

"Can you call the airport?" Rafael asked Johnny. "Ask them for help. Tell them our location."

"No!" Johnny yelled over the noise. "We have no power. The radio is out."

"Try anyway! Please!" Antonio screamed.

Johnny got on the radio. "Mayday! Mayday!"

It didn't work. The radio was dead. No one heard them. Johnny tried to fly the plane. It didn't help. The plane fell. They were going to crash!

"Can we make it?" Rafael asked Johnny.

"I think so. I think it will be okay. I will crash land. We are over the desert. There are no trees. The ground is flat. But it will be scary. Hold on tight!" Johnny said.

Rafael looked at his kids. They looked scared. The plane fell. It fell fast. Johnny tried to steer. He tried to slow the plane down. The ground came closer and closer.

"Hold on tight!" Johnny yelled again.

Lilia closed her eyes. Antonio screamed. Franco held his breath. The plane hit the ground. It hit the ground fast. It was over. They were on land. They made it!

"Are you guys okay?" Rafael asked.

One by one, they replied.

"Yup," said Franco.

"Alive, but scared," Antonio cried.

"I'm okay," called Lilia.

"How about you Johnny?" asked Rafael.

"I'm fine," Johnny said. "But the plane isn't. We can't fly out of here."

"No one knows where we are," Lilia sobbed.

"Yeah," said Antonio. "The radio broke. No one heard our Mayday!"

"True," Rafael said. "But they will know we crashed. They will find us."

"What do we do now?" asked Franco.

Johnny looked around. He needed a plan. They were in the desert. He knew the desert. He knew they'd be okay. They had to be careful. But they would be okay.

The desert was an odd place. It was hot all day. It was cold all night. They'd stay out of the sun in the day. They'd try to keep warm in the night.

There was some food in the plane. But there was no water. They needed water.

Everyone got out of the plane.

They stood in the sand. The desert was hot! The sun was bright.

"Wow!" Antonio said. "It is hot out here!"

"Yeah, we need to find water," Johnny said. "Grab water bottles. We can fill them."

"Where is the water?" Lilia asked.

Johnny pointed. He pointed to a big mountain.

"Up there," he said.

They all looked. The mountain was far. It was big. It wouldn't be easy. But they needed water. They could be lost for days.

"We'll go in the morning," Rafael said. "Let's get some rest."

Chapter 3

Johnny was right. The desert was odd. It was cold at night. Rafael built a fire. They sat around it.

"Hey Johnny," asked Lilia. "How do you know about the desert?"

"I am Navajo," he said. "My family is from this desert."

"That's cool," said Antonio. "So you know this area."

"Well, no. The Navajos had

villages all over the area. But I grew up in San Francisco. My great-grandpa Billy Two Nose grew up in the desert."

"That's a funny name," Antonio said. "How did he get it?"

"That's a long story," Johnny laughed. "Billy *sensed* things before they happened."

"Like ESP?" asked Franco.

"Yes. Just like ESP," Johnny said. "Billy saved his village once. He had a bad feeling. He *sensed* danger. He told everyone. Some thought he was crazy. Some listened. A lot got ready to fight. Then they were attacked! It was a long fight. They won! Thanks to Billy Two Nose. But they would have lost. Billy saved the village. He was a hero."

"Your great-grandpa was cool," Antonio said. "But what's up with his name?"

"The village had a party for him," Johnny replied. "The chief called him Billy Two Nose. Because Billy could smell trouble. One nose couldn't smell like that. You needed two."

"I am glad you're with us," Lilia said.

"Me too," said Johnny. "Now get some sleep! We have a long hike tomorrow."

Chapter 4

Everyone woke up early. It was 5:00 a.m. The sun wasn't out yet. But it was getting hot. They went to find water. And they needed to walk fast. The sun would be out soon. It would get even hotter.

It took an hour. But they made it to the mountain. Everyone was tired.

"Let's rest," Johnny said. "We have to climb the mountain. The water is at the top."

It was a good idea. They all needed rest.

Antonio sat on a rock. He looked scared. "What if we can't find water?" he asked. "We should have stayed in The Heights. Some vacation!"

"There is water up there," Johnny said. He ignored Antonio's bad mood.

"I hope so," Franco said. "I'm thirsty!"

"I'm thirsty and hot!" Lilia whined.

"We all are," Rafael said. "But Johnny is smart. He knows the desert. We will find water."

Everyone hoped he was right. They wouldn't last long without water.

"Let's get started," Johnny said.

They started walking up. They saw a lot of animals. They saw birds.

And rabbits. And mice.

"I think you're right Johnny," Antonio said. "I bet there's water up here."

"Why do you think that?" Johnny asked.

"I see a lot of animals. Animals need water too. Water must be close," said Antonio.

"Good thinking!" Franco said.

"You're right," said Johnny. "Water has to be close."

Antonio was excited. He ran ahead. He wanted to find water first.

"Keep close," Rafael said. "You don't want to get lost."

They were 100 feet up. Franco looked down. He could see the plane. It looked far.

"Hey!" Lilia yelled. "Water! I found it!"

Everyone ran to Lilia. They all smiled. Even Antonio. He didn't care that Lilia was first. He just wanted a drink. He was very thirsty. They were all thirsty!

They all took a drink. It was good!

"I've never liked water this much. It tastes better than soda!" Antonio said.

They all laughed.

"Okay guys," said Rafael. "Take another drink. Then fill up the bottles. We have to head back. The sun is hot. We need to get to the plane."

They all filled the bottles. Rafael was right. The walk back was long. And it was hot.

Chapter 5

The walk back was slow. It was hot.
The sun was out. At least they had
water! Johnny let them take a break.
Johnny looked at the desert. It was big.
He saw something. It was far. It looked
like a cloud. But it wasn't in the sky.

"Come on," he said. "We have to
get back. We have to get there fast!"

Johnny looked scared. Rafael
didn't like it.

"What's wrong?" Rafael asked.

"See that?" asked Johnny.

Johnny pointed. The Silvas looked. They saw the cloud. It was strange.

"What is it?" Lilia asked. "It looks like a cloud."

"It is a cloud," said Johnny. "It's a cloud made of sand. It's a sandstorm."

"Wow! I've never seen a sandstorm. It looks cool," said Lilia.

"It's very dangerous," said Johnny. "We have to get moving."

Everyone ran. They ran fast. The cloud got bigger. It was moving fast! The plane was not far.

They almost made it.

The wind blew hard. It blew sand into their faces. It blew sand into their eyes. They covered their eyes.

The sand stung.

"Keep your eyes closed. Grab the person in front of you. Hold on to them. And stay together!" Johnny yelled.

The Silvas did what Johnny said. Johnny was right. It was windy. It was hard to walk. But they made it to the plane. The wind hit the plane. The plane shook hard.

"That was crazy!" Franco said. He was breathing hard.

"Yeah. Good thing Johnny's here. He saw the sandstorm," said Rafael.

"I was lucky," Johnny said.

"No," said Antonio. "You were great. You *saw* the storm. You're like your great-grandpa."

"We can call *you* Johnny Two Nose!" Lilia said.

Everyone laughed.

After the sandstorm, no one could see outside. Johnny opened the door. They stepped outside. The plane was covered in sand.

Johnny looked worried. "It's hard to see the plane. We need to dig it out. Rescue crews need to see our plane."

They cleaned off the plane. Everyone helped. They dug it out of the sand. It took a long time.

"That was hard," said Antonio. "That was a lot of sand!"

"Well, we are in the desert!" Lilia said.

"True," Antonio said.

"Craziest vacation ever," said Franco.

Chapter 6

It was dark. Everyone was tired. It was a long day. They slept outside. The air was cool. The sand was soft.

"I wish I had pizza," Franco sighed.

"Stop. Don't even talk about food!" Lilia said. "I am so hungry."

"We'll look for food tomorrow," Johnny said.

"What kind of food?" asked Franco.

"Cactus plants. It's not pizza. But it's okay. You'll like it," said Johnny.

"Shhh, kids. Go to sleep," Rafael said.

Later, Rafael heard something. It was dark. He tried to see. Then he woke up Johnny.

"I heard something. I don't know what it was," said Rafael.

Johnny sat up. He listened. He looked around.

"We have to get up. Let's go to the plane," Johnny said.

Rafael woke up his kids. They all went back to the plane.

"What is it?" Rafael asked.

"Coyotes," Johnny said. "We'll be safer in the plane."

They all went back to sleep.

Johnny woke up early. He looked out the window. He didn't see any coyotes. Outside there were tracks in the sand. They were coyote tracks. A lot of coyote tracks. There were about 12 coyotes. Good thing Rafael heard them.

"Hey Johnny," Rafael said. "Wow, look at all those tracks. Are they coyote tracks?"

"Yes," Johnny said. "We are safe now. They won't come out in the day. It's too hot."

Chapter 7

The three Silva kids woke up. They got out of the plane.

"I'm hungry," Antonio said. "Can we find some cactus now?"

"Sure. Antonio and Franco come with me. Lilia and Rafael stay here. You need to make a fire. Grab what you can. Make a big pile of stuff. Light it. Smoke can be seen from the sky. Rescue planes will see it. They will look for us," said Johnny.

Rafael did what Johnny said. They were glad he was with them.

"Come on boys," said Johnny.

Johnny, Franco, and Antonio left. Rafael and Lilia waved.

"I hope they aren't gone long," Rafael said.

The desert was hot. Antonio hoped they found the cactus fast. They walked for an hour. Johnny saw something. It was a big cactus!

"That's it!" Johnny yelled.

They ran to the cactus. It was big. Johnny cut the cactus. Antonio couldn't wait to eat. They had to carry pieces to the plane.

Then Franco saw something. It was a hole. The hole was big. It was

about 8 feet deep. Franco slipped.
He was in the hole! Then he heard a
noise. It was a hissing sound.

Antonio looked into the hole. He
saw Franco.

"Franco, are you okay?" Antonio
asked.

Franco was scared. He couldn't
move. Snakes! There were 20 snakes
hissing at him. The snakes looked
mad. Franco didn't know what to do.

"Snakes!" Franco yelled. "And
they are mad."

Johnny looked into the hole. He
put his arm in.

"Grab my arm," Johnny said.

Franco looked at Johnny. He
grabbed his arm. But the snakes
were fast. One bit his leg. Franco

screamed. Johnny pulled him out of the hole. The snake held on. Johnny hit the snake. It let go.

"It bit me!" Franco screamed. "Am I going to die?"

"No," said Johnny.

Johnny looked at Antonio. "Run to the plane. Get the first aid kit. There is a drug in it. It's for snakebites. Go as fast as you can. Franco's life depends on it!"

Chapter 8

Antonio ran fast. The desert was hot.
He was thirsty. He had to get the
drug. It would save his big brother.
Johnny watched Antonio run. He
waited with Franco.

"Be still," Johnny said. "Antonio
will be back soon. He will have the
drug. You will be okay."

"Okay, Johnny," Franco said. "It
hurts. I'm glad Antonio is a fast

runner. Don't tell him I said that."

Franco was sweating. He could feel the poison in his leg.

Lilia saw Antonio. She saw him running. She saw he was alone. She was worried.

"Dad!" Lilia yelled. "Antonio's back. And he's alone."

Rafael knew something was wrong. Johnny would never leave Antonio alone.

"What's wrong?" Rafael asked.

"It's Franco. He fell into a hole. Lots of snakes! One bit him. He needs a special drug. It's in the plane," said Antonio.

Rafael froze. He was scared. He knew snakebites were bad.

"How far away is he?" Rafael asked.

"A mile," said Antonio. "We have to get back fast."

Antonio ran to the plane. He found the first aid kit. He grabbed the drug.

"Come on Lilia," Rafael said. "We'll go too."

Rafael grabbed water. He gave it to Antonio. Antonio took a big gulp.

"Quick," said Rafael. "We don't have much time."

They started running. They had to get to Franco. They had to get there fast.

Franco was in pain. He was sweating a lot. He needed the drug soon.

Johnny saw Antonio. He was ahead of Rafael and Lilia.

"Here," Antonio said. He gave Johnny the drug.

Johnny grabbed it. He stuck the needle in Franco's leg.

"I hope that worked," Antonio said.

"It will," said Johnny. "You got it fast. You saved his life."

Johnny picked up Franco. He put him over his shoulders. At 17, Franco was tall. But Johnny was really tall.

"Let's head back," Johnny said.

They walked back to the plane. They saw Rafael and Lilia. Rafael ran to Johnny.

"How is he?" Rafael asked. He looked worried.

"He's going to be okay. Thanks to

Antonio," said Johnny. "Your sons are brave."

Franco looked at his dad. He was feeling better. The drug did work fast.

Lilia gave him water. "Drink up," she said.

"Thanks," Franco said. "I need some."

Franco took a sip. He gave Antonio the water. "Thanks Antonio. I'll never call you slow again!" he said.

Everyone laughed.

Chapter 9

They made it to the plane. Rafael
made a bed for Franco. He wanted
him to rest. Lilia sat next to Franco.
She made sure he felt okay. She
helped him play Antonio's DS.

Rafael knew the kids were scared.
This wasn't a vacation! He knew Ana
would be mad.

"Don't worry. Franco will be okay.
He got the drug fast. He just needs

rest," Johnny said.

The Silvas felt better. They knew Johnny was right.

Franco fell asleep. The others got more stuff for the fire. It was almost dark. It had been another long day!

"We will light the fire tomorrow. They won't look for us tonight. It's too dark," said Johnny.

"Hey Johnny," Antonio said. "Do you still have the cactus? I forgot about it. And I'm still hungry!"

"I forgot about it too!" Lilia said.

"So did I," said Johnny.

Johnny gave everyone cactus. They all ate.

"It's not pizza," Antonio said. "But it's not that bad!"

"I've had worse," said Rafael.

"Me too," Johnny said. "In the army I ate rats! And bugs!"

"Gross!" Lilia sniffed. She stuck out her tongue.

"Yeah, it was gross," said Johnny. "This is a feast."

They all laughed.

They woke up Franco. "Why are you laughing?" he asked.

"Franco! You're up," said Lilia. "How are you feeling?"

"I'm okay. Just hungry," Franco said.

"He must be better. He's hungry," Johnny said.

"Franco is always hungry," Lilia said. "He plays football. What do you want cactus or rat?"

Franco looked at Lilia. "Rat?" he

said. "Gross! Give me some cactus!"

Everyone laughed again.

Johnny heard a noise. "Okay guys," he said. "Back inside the plane. It's dark now. We don't want the coyotes getting us!"

They got in the plane fast.

"I think we'll get rescued tomorrow," Johnny said.

"Okay Johnny Two Nose. I believe you. You're always right," said Lilia.

Chapter 10

The coyotes did return! They walked
up to the plane. Good thing Johnny
made them get inside. The coyotes
were scary. They had red eyes. Their
teeth were sharp.

Lilia looked out the window.
There were a lot of coyotes. One
looked right at her. It growled. Lilia
looked away.

"I'm so glad we're in here!" Lilia cried.

"They'll be gone by morning," Johnny said. "The sun is too hot for them."

"Good! A snakebite is bad. I don't want a coyote bite too," Franco joked.

Johnny got up early. He got out of the plane. Then he heard a growl. The coyote pack was still there!

Johnny ran back. The coyotes followed him. And they were fast. One tried to bite his arm. But Johnny was fast too. He made it to the plane. He closed the door hard. He woke up the Silvas.

"What's wrong?" Rafael asked.

"We have a problem. The coyotes

never left. They are outside!" said
Johnny.

"Uh-oh! How many are there?"
asked Lilia.

"About 12. They look hungry,"
Johnny said. "We need to scare them
away."

"We need to light the fire," said
Rafael. "The rescue planes need it to
see us."

They didn't have anything to
scare the coyotes. They needed a
plan.

Franco looked out the window.
He heard a noise. "What's that?" he
asked.

The noise got louder.

Johnny heard it too. "It's a plane.
I bet it's looking for us," he said.

"I wish we could light that fire. But the plane isn't buried now. Maybe they'll see us," Rafael said.

"I hope so," Johnny said.

Everyone looked out the windows. They looked at the coyotes. They looked for the plane.

"The plane didn't see us," Antonio said. "I can't hear it anymore."

Everyone looked scared. Even Johnny. They had no food. The coyotes waited for them. That rescue plane was their only chance.

Two hours went by. Franco heard another noise. It was a different noise. It was louder. It was a chopper! The plane had seen them. They were going to be rescued!

The chopper blew a lot of sand. It

was loud. The sand and noise scared the coyotes. They ran.

The chopper landed. The pilot had water and food. Johnny and the Silvas ate and drank. They were happy they weren't coyote food!

"It took us a long time to find you. The storm blew you off track," the pilot said.

"It's okay," said Lilia. "We're glad you're here now!"

"You came just in time," Antonio said.

Everyone got in the chopper. The flight was smooth. They saw a lot of sand. The desert was huge!

Then they landed. Jack Wheeler was there. So was a doctor. The doctor looked at Franco's leg.

"What do you think?" Rafael
asked. "Will he be okay?"

"He'll be fine," the doctor said.
"That drug saved his life."

Jack Wheeler was happy. The
Silvas were safe. He had been
worried. He knew Johnny would
help them. But he was still upset.
California was his idea.

Rafael knew his kids were going
to miss Johnny. He knew they
wouldn't have survived without him.
Johnny had become a good friend.
Rafael thanked him for saving his
kids.

Franco and Antonio also thanked
Johnny. They told him they'd never
forget him. Then Lilia ran over to
Johnny. She threw her arms around

his neck.

"Bye Johnny Two Nose!" Lilia cried. "You are a hero. Just like your great-grandpa."

"Now," said Rafael to the kids, "we really need to call your mom. She knows we're okay. But she will want to talk to us."

"Uh-oh," said Antonio. "Do you think she'll ever let us leave the Heights again?"

Everyone laughed. Not likely.